HANS DE BEER was born in 1957 in Muiden, a small town near Amsterdam, in Holland. He began to draw when he went to school, mostly when the lessons got too boring. In college he studied history, but he was drawing so many pictures during the lectures that he decided to become an artist. He went on to study illustration at the Rietveld Academy of Art in Amsterdam.

Hans de Beer's first book, *Little Polar Bear*, was very popular around the world. The book has been published in eighteen languages. Hans had so much fun illustrating picture books that he did more of them. He likes to draw polar bears, cats, walruses, elephants, and moles. His books have received many prizes, among them the first prize from an international jury of children in Bologna, Italy.

MIX
Paper from
responsible sources
FSC® C043106
FSC
www.fsc.org

Copyright © 2018 by NordSüd Verlag AG, CH-8050 Zürich, Switzerland.
First published in Switzerland under the title *Kleiner Eisbär – Lars und die verschwundenen Fische*.
English text copyright © 2018 by NorthSouth Books, Inc., New York 10016.
Translated by David Henry Wilson.

First published in the United States, Great Britain, Canada, Australia, and New Zealand in 2018
by NorthSouth Books, Inc., an imprint of NordSüd Verlag AG, CH-8005 Zürich, Switzerland.

Distributed in the United States by NorthSouth Books, Inc., New York 10016.
Library of Congress Cataloging-in-Publication Data is available.

ISBN: 978-0-7358-4297-7 (trade edition)
1 3 5 7 9 • 10 8 6 4 2

Printed in Germany by Grafisches Centrum Cuno GmbH & Co. KG, 2017

www.northsouth.com

Hans de Beer

LITTLE POLAR BEAR

Takes a Stand

North
South

Spring had arrived at the North Pole. Lars, the little polar bear, poked his nose out of his den and sniffed the air. "It's nice and warm!" he cried.

"Much too warm!" grumbled Lars's father. "It's even warmer than last year."

Just at that moment, a helicopter flew over their heads.

"Yet another one of those ear-splitting ice-shakers!" he said.

"This heat isn't just melting the ice," said Lars's mother, looking worried. "It's also bringing more and more humans here. For weeks now they've been going to the fishing bay."

Lars pricked his ears. The fishing bay was not far away. Last summer he and his father had often gone there to fish. Lars decided that he would go and see the bay in the morning.

The next day Lars set out on his way. The spring air tickled his nostrils, and he was almost bursting with curiosity. The fact is, he was not allowed to go there alone. But what harm could there be? He just wanted to have a quick look. After all, it's not every day that you can see humans.

If he went along the coast, it would take quite a long time to get to the bay. But Lars knew from his trips with his father that it was much quicker to go through a crack in an iceberg. The thought of crawling all alone through the dark and narrow passage was a bit scary, but Lars took a deep breath and stepped inside.

As he crawled along between the walls of the iceberg, he didn't see anything unusual.

The bay was not as frozen as it had been last year, but all the same he couldn't see any humans. He knew that the bay was part of a strait and was simply overflowing with fish.

After all that walking, the little polar bear was hungry. He hurried down to the shore. Strange! There were no fish swimming around in the water. Last year, he had only needed to dip his paw in the sea for a second or two, and straightaway he'd caught a fish. But now there was not a single one to be seen.

After looking around for a long time, Lars finally spotted a few little fish down in the depths of the sea. Without his father there, the water seemed especially cold and dark, but his hunger was greater than his fear. With a skillful jump, he dived into the water, just as his father had shown him.

At last he managed to catch a fish. But then he suddenly realized that he was not alone. A little seal was also trying to catch a fish, and from above came a bird that was doing the same thing. The three of them all looked at one another in surprise.

When they climbed out of the water, each of them nibbled away at their meager meal.

"I think it's pretty stupid the way you go splashing around like that," said the seal to the bird. "You scare all the fish away!"

"So you're blaming it all on me, are you?" squawked the bird. "The fact is, it's strangers like this polar bear that are frightening the fish away."

"But there have always been enough fish here for everyone!" protested Lars.

The quarrel was interrupted by the sound of a horn, and then a huge container ship made its way across the narrow bay. In the wake of the ship, the water surged and splashed, and blocks of ice crashed into one another. The bird let out a sigh. "Ah, you see, that's the reason there aren't any fish here now. It's because of all the ships that have started rumbling through the bay."

The bird was a tern, and her name was Isa.

Isa pointed toward the shore with her beak.

"A few weeks ago, the humans built a radio station over there, and a bit farther on they threw a large buoy into the sea. Since then, these big ships have been churning everything up, and almost all the fish have disappeared."

"With all the activity and noise, life underwater has become unbearable!" sighed Robbie the seal.

"You're right. And we'd better do something about it! After all, it's our fishing bay!" said Lars. "Come on, let's go and have a look at this radio station. I might have an idea what to do once we're there."

The three of them swam across the bay. Isa kept Lars company, because Bertie was very fast. He'd already swum there and back three times before the little polar bear managed to reach halfway.

"Better to be careful than rushed," said Lars.

But when they had to climb uphill toward the radio station, it was Bertie who got left behind.

"Maybe too careful!" laughed Lars. "Why don't you just stay here and keep watch, Bertie. Isa and I can manage this on our own."

However, when they got to the radio station, Lars and Isa found their way blocked by a high metal fence covered in barbed wire.

"Oh dear!" gulped Lars. "I'll never be able to get over that."

Luckily, Isa had an idea. "Wait here," she said. "I'll be right back." And away she flew.

After a few minutes, Lars suddenly heard a loud screeching and flapping. When he looked up, there were flocks of birds swarming all over the radio station.

With their sharp beaks, they pecked the posts and panels and walls and windows to pieces.

In no time at all, there was nothing left of the radio station except a smoldering pile of ruins.

Isa flew back to where Lars was waiting, and then together they rejoined Bertie.

"Unbelievable!" gasped Lars. "I've never seen anything like it!"

"Many beaks make light work!" Isa laughed.

"Right! And now for the buoy!" cried Lars and Bertie.

But the buoy was made of solid steel, and it was much harder to wreck than the radio station had been.

It was also rocking around in the water, which made Isa and Lars feel rather seasick.

"Just fix your eyes on the horizon," said Bertie, "and you won't feel sick anymore."

Lars had a thought. "If the buoy is rocking, doesn't that mean it's floating on the water?" he asked. "But how can something so heavy float?" He looked around.

Then he discovered a hatch. With a lot of grunting and groaning and pulling and pushing, he finally managed to open it.

"It's empty in here," cried the little polar bear, his voice echoing in the hollow space. "That's why the buoy is able to float on the water."

Toot toot! A gigantic ship came sailing past. The three friends took cover behind the buoy, though it was bobbing wildly up and down.

"Come and look at this!" called Bertie when the ship was a safe distance away. "When I dived, I found a cable under the buoy. That's what it's tied to. I think I've got an idea."

And with a splash, the seal disappeared under the water.

Not long afterward the bay was swarming with seals, big and little—all friends or relatives of Bertie's. Now Lars could see what Bertie was planning.

"Great idea!" he said.

When Bertie gave the signal, all the seals dived. Together they pulled on the cable, and slowly the buoy sank deeper and deeper into the sea until the open hatch finally dipped below the level of the water. Then everything happened very quickly. The buoy filled up and plunged like a ton of bricks down to the bottom of the sea.

"Slam dunk, the buoy is sunk!" cheered Lars and Isa.

The work was complete. Without the radio station and the signals from the buoy, ships could no longer pass through the strait. Lars and his friends watched as the helicopter circled overhead for the last time, surveying the damage. Then with a roar it disappeared over the horizon.

"Bye-bye, ice-shaker!" laughed Lars.

And so at last there was peace again in the fishing bay. The ice slowly joined up again, and soon there were shoals of fish dashing around in the sea. There was more than enough food for everyone.

All through the summer, Lars, Bertie, and Isa met at least once a week in the bay to enjoy a feast of fish.